PUSH-PULL MORNING

Dog-Powered Poems About Matter and Energy

By Lisa Westberg Peters

Illustrated by Serge Bloch

WORDSONG

AN IMPRINT OF ASTRA BOOKS FOR YOUNG READERS

New York

Contents

Stuff in Common

My new dog has one wet nose.
Me? No.

My new dog has two floppy ears.
Me? No.

My new dog has four paws and
sixteen clicky claws.
Me? Nope.

But—

my new dog
(with her nose, ears, paws, and clicky claws)
is made of
zillions of wiggly molecules and
jillions of jiggly atoms.

Me, too!

My new dog and I
are made of the SAME
wiggly-jiggly stuff.
That's why we're already
super-duper friends!

Matter

Friendship

Phase-Crazy Dog

My amazing dog
goes through phases.
She is like a Solid
whenever she eats dinner.

She has
a definite dog shape
and a definite dog size
and a definite dog desire
to be left alone.

My amazing dog
is like a Liquid
whenever she sleeps in her basket.

She has a definite dog size,
but she can pour that dog size
into a basket shape.

My amazing dog
is like a Gas
whenever she chases flies.

She leaps! She jumps!
She's everywhere at once!
My amazing, phase-crazy dog
fills Aunty Rosa's living room!

SOLID

LIQUID

Phases of Matter

6

GAS

Dog in Motion

My squirrel-chasing dog
can run straight to the tree
and round and round the tree.

The squirrel can run
straight up the tree and
round and round the branches.

My squirrel-chasing dog
can run back and forth
from me to the tree.

The squirrel could run
back and forth, fast and slow,
up, down, and round and round
all afternoon.

My tongue-hanging dog
pants, pauses, and pretends
not to care about squirrels.

The squirrel doesn't pause,
doesn't pant, and
doesn't pretend anything.

I don't run.
I just sit, pet my tired dog,
and smile.

Motion

8

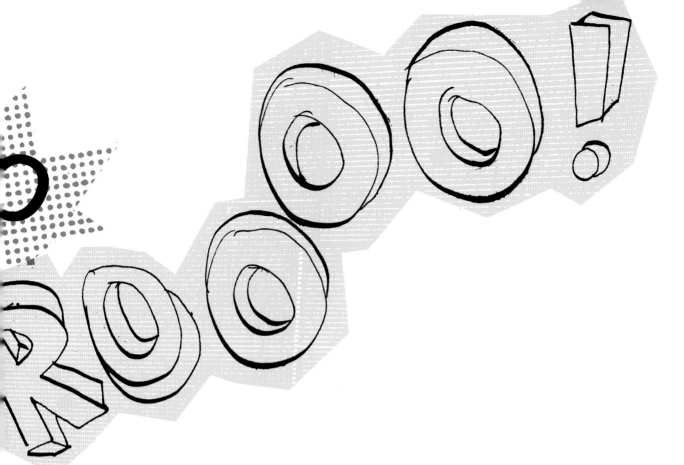

The Howl of the Hunt

My city dog can sleep
through the *BZZZZ*
of a dozen lawn mowers
and the *WHOOOOSH*
of nearby street sweepers.
But when a fire engine's siren
goes *WOOOO* and
vibrates the air on our street,
my city dog hears
a wild dog on a hunt.

ROOOO! howls my city dog.
Can I come TOOOO?
And will there be FOOOOD?

Sound

Push-Pull Morning

My let's-go-for-a-walk dog *pulls* on her leash.
Aunty Rosa *pushes* open our back door.

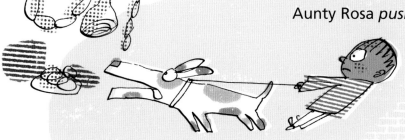

We pass the butcher's big display window.
I *pull* my dog away from the mounds of meat.

Aunty Rosa *pulls* open the door to the vet's.
We have to *push* my dog into the room.

The vet *pushes* his fingers into my dog's tummy.
My dog *pulls* back her lip.

The vet just smiles and *pulls* out fresh dog tags.
My dog *pushes* against my leg. I *pull* her close.

We finally leave. I *push* open the clinic's door.
My let's-get-out-of-here dog *pulls* on her leash.

We pass our neighbor's big picture window.
I *pull* my dog away from their cowardly cat.

We are finally home. I *pull* open our back door.
My let's-have-a-snack dog trots around the kitchen,

Force

pushing for a treat, *pulling* for a treat . . .
until I say, "OK!"

What Will It Take? #1

My resting dog
  wants to keep resting
    all afternoon.

    What will it take
  to make her wake
up and play with me?

One nudge?
  Not enough.
    Two pokes?
      Almost enough.
Three tickles?

    Ha!

14

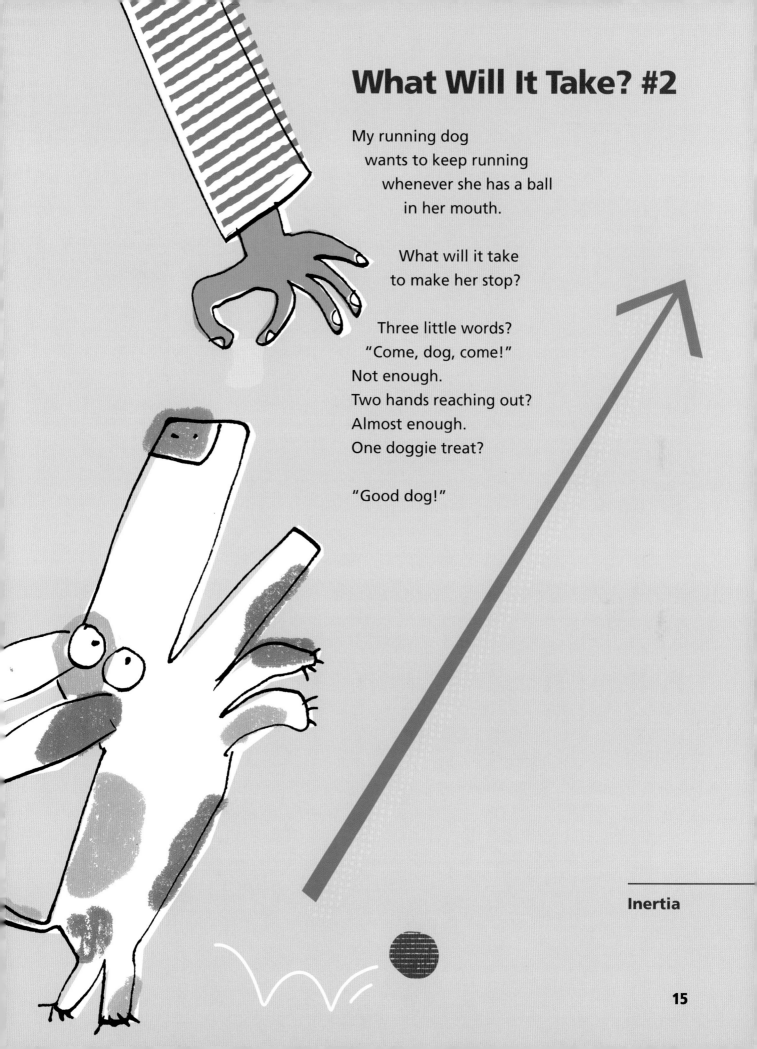

What Will It Take? #2

My running dog
    wants to keep running
        whenever she has a ball
            in her mouth.

    What will it take
    to make her stop?

    Three little words?
    "Come, dog, come!"
    Not enough.
    Two hands reaching out?
    Almost enough.
    One doggie treat?

    "Good dog!"

Inertia

Falling Toward Earth #1

My scaredy-cat dog
refuses to slide down the
super slide at the Totally Wacky
Fun Park. So Aunty Rosa and I climb
up the stairs and sit on two little blankets.
"One, two, three, let's go!" We're falling down
the super slide—faster and faster—"*WHEEEEEE!*"

Falling Toward Earth #2

Oh! My eager-beaver dog is waiting at the bottom of the slide. We might crash! I wish Aunty Rosa and I could fall UP instead of DOWN, but the only way we can fall is DOWN. We get closer and closer then *WHOA! OOOOOMPH!* And a big happy lick!

Gravity

Attracted to a Magnet

My patient dog
waits
and
woofs
and
wonders
why the dog bone stuck
to Aunty Rosa's fridge
doesn't fall.

Magnetism

Light Stops

My furry dog
is like a red light for the sun's light.

Light stops.
It can't go through my dog.

She jumps, she bounces,
she sniffs, she pounces
at her shifting shadows.

Heat Goes

My furry dog
is like a green light for the sun's heat.

Heat goes
right through my dog.
She can't stop it.

Her tongue drops,
her ears flop,
even her tail stops wagging.

My stop-and-go dog
shuffles into the shade
where she happily trades
both light and heat for
water and me.

Energy

Extra Electrons #1

My happy dog likes almost everything except
storms.
Thunder-
clouds
bring
electrons.
The clouds wrap up those electrical charges
in
jagged
lightning
packages
and
toss them down to the trees
or
the
ground
or
anything
else
that seems low on electrons.
My
poor
dog
whimpers.
She seems low on lots of things—
happiness,
courage,
maybe
even
electrons.
We turn on the lamp and read
until
the
storm
clouds
vanish.

Extra Electrons #2

My generous dog
   gives me electrons
      on cool, dry days.

     She rolls around on the carpet.
     Her fur picks up electrons
       until she is excessively negative.

      She gives me a nose kiss
       PLUS electrons.

       Zap!

      I try to look stuffed with electrons.
    "I don't want any more!" I shout.

      I just want a nose kiss
       MINUS electrons,
         but . . .

       ZAP!

Electricity

24

Remembering Friction

My stinky dog

remembers friction
when I tell her it's time for a bath.

"Let's go," I say, but
she digs her claws into the carpet.
My stinky dog knows that

Carpet + Claws = Friction.

I have to carry her
all the way to the bathtub.

I start to scrub with soapy fingers,
but my dog knows that

Soap + Fingers = Not Enough Friction

and she escapes!
"Come back, stinky dog!"

Forgetting Friction

My still-stinky dog

forgets about friction
when she wants a doggie treat.

"First you need a bath," I tell her.
She tries to dig her claws
into the kitchen floor, but

Claws + Smooth Floor = Not Much Friction.

"Good try, stinky dog."

I lift her into the tub and scrub her
with my two new brushes.

Soap + Scrub Brushes = Just Enough Friction

to wash a very dirty dog.

"All done, clean dog.
Time for a treat!"

Friction

Racing Through Space

My running-partner dog and I
raced down the block
this morning.
She ran much faster.

My running-partner dog and I
raced in the park
this afternoon.
I won by a nose.

My resting-partner dog and I
are relaxing now, but
we're still racing through space
on our spinning, orbiting planet.
Earth, dog, and I: a three-way tie!

Relative Motion

Reflecting on a Star

My favorite dog
and I stare at the stars
when it gets dark.

We wonder
why the North Star
isn't twinkling tonight.
Is it too high?
Is it too bright?

It doesn't seem right,
a star with no twinkle.

My dog tilts her head
to figure out why.
Her curious eyes
catch the light
of a star-filled sky.
Finally I see it.
How did I miss it?

The twinkle of *my* star.

Reflection of Light

Our Place in the Universe

My cosmic dog and I
are just
specks
in outer space.

We live in an ordinary spot
on a rocky planet,
which spins around an ordinary star
in an ordinary galaxy.

But at bedtime tonight
in the story-time chair
with Aunty Rosa,

we are in the center
of our universe.

Paradox

Dog-Powered Notes

Stuff in Common

Matter is the physical "stuff" of the world that has weight (mass) and occupies space.

Everything around us—balls and bats, kids and dogs, water and air—is made of matter. All matter is made of atoms or combinations of atoms, which are called molecules. Atoms and molecules are too small for the human eye to see. Even in solid things like books or rocks, these particles are in constant motion because they all have energy. We can't see the motion because the particles are too small. Atoms themselves are made of even smaller particles called protons, neutrons, and electrons.

Matter has features we can observe, like size, shape, color, and texture. It also has characteristics that relate to how it changes when it interacts with other matter. For example, the iron in a chain turns into something else—rust—when it sits too long in a puddle of water.

Phase-Crazy Dog

Phases of matter are the different forms matter can take. Matter can be a solid like ice, a liquid like water, or a gas like water vapor. Solids, liquids, and gases are the three common phases of matter.

A solid object holds its shape; the atoms are packed tightly and move very little. In liquids, the atoms are not as close and move freely to take the shape of their container. In gases, the atoms are relatively far apart, and move more and faster than the atoms in solids or liquids. Gases fill whatever containers they are in, no matter the volume or shape.

Dog in Motion

Motion is a change in position over time.

Objects and bodies can move in many ways, such as forward, backward, up, down, straight ahead or in a curve, and at different speeds. Everything in the universe is in constant motion. Even an apparently motionless child is moving. On a small scale, a child's molecules and atoms are always vibrating. On a large scale, the child's home, the planet earth, is always spinning and always revolving around the sun.

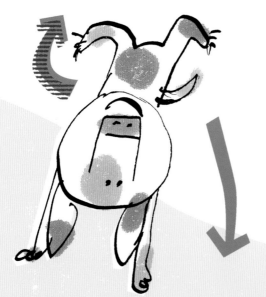

The Howl of the Hunt

Sound is a vibration that travels through a solid, liquid, or gas and can be heard or felt by living organisms.

Hearing sound happens in many steps. For example, a siren causes the air molecules around it to move back and forth, creating a wave. The wave vibrates the molecules entering a dog's ear. The ear turns the vibrations into electrical signals, and then those signals are carried by nerves from the dog's ear to her brain. To a dog, the siren sounds like another dog howling. The dog often howls back because dogs once hunted in packs, and they signaled to each other by howling. People used to think dogs howled at sirens because the noise hurt their ears, but if dogs were in pain, they would show other behaviors like tucking their tails or running and hiding.

Push-Pull Morning

Force is an influence that tends to change the motion of a physical body.

To *push* is to apply force on an object so that the object moves away from the source of the force. To *pull* is to apply force on an object so that the object moves toward the source of the force. Pushes and pulls can be strong or weak and can have different directions. We push and pull on things every day. Sometimes the closed door of a store will even have a sign telling us whether to push or pull to make the door open.

What Will It Take? #1, #2

Inertia (in-ER-sha) is the tendency of an object to stay at rest or keep moving in a straight line unless an outside force acts on it.

It seems odd that something as simple as motion should have laws, but more than three hundred years ago, an English mathematician named Isaac Newton discovered laws that help us understand motion. The first law tells us that an object tends to stay still or keep moving in a straight line if it isn't being pushed or pulled by a force. For example, a ball rolling through the grass won't keep rolling forever. It will gradually slow down and stop because the grass resists the forward motion of the ball. A child's tickles and promises of doggie treats have a force of their own, but probably not the kind of force Sir Newton had in mind.

Falling Toward Earth #1, #2

Gravity is the force that attracts physical bodies toward each other. It's the force that pulls us toward the center of the earth. Gravity makes us slide down, rather than up, the slides at the playground and fall back to the earth after we jump.

About four hundred years ago, an Italian scientist named Galileo Galilei studied motion and gravity. He rolled a ball down ramps to learn how much an object speeds up as it falls. He also discovered that gravity pulls all objects toward the earth at the same rate whether they're light or heavy. And yet, on the earth, some things like feathers fall more slowly than hammers. That's because molecules of air resist, or slow down, the fall of very light objects. When the Apollo 15 astronauts landed on the moon in 1971, they showed that feathers and hammers fall at the same rate where there is very little air.

Attracted to a Magnet

Magnetism is a force produced by a moving electric charge.

Magnetism seems like magic. Something invisible attracts or repels two objects. But long ago, scientists learned that magnetism is as simple—and complicated—as wiggling, jiggling electrons. In many substances, there isn't any organization to the way electrons wiggle and jiggle, so any magnetic properties are cancelled out. But in certain elements like iron, the motions of its electrons can line up to create a magnetic field. The dog bone magnet you buy at the pet store has a magnetic field. When you put the magnet on the refrigerator door, its magnetic field causes the iron in the door at that particular spot to become magnetized. That's why it is attracted to the door.

Light Stops, Heat Goes

Energy is an abstract idea and hard to define, but scientists usually describe energy as the ability to do work. Energy moves through everything in many ways.

Energy is carried from the sun to the earth by sunshine. And sunshine can be broken down into three different parts: visible light waves, infrared waves, and ultraviolet (UV) waves. Visible light waves do the work of making things visible to us. They bounce off the surface of solid objects like a dog, allowing us to see the dog. Infrared waves make up most of the energy from the sun. They do the work of heating up the dog. The dog absorbs much of the infrared and that adds energy to the dog's molecules so that the molecules vibrate even faster. The extra motion of the molecules heats up the dog. Not all UV waves make it to the earth's surface. They are blocked by our atmosphere, which is good for us because UV waves do the work of creating sunburn—even on a dog.

Extra Electrons #1, #2

Electricity is a form of energy caused by tiny charged particles such as electrons.

Lightning still isn't completely understood, but we do know lightning is a giant spark of electricity. It's caused by electrically charged particles that attract and repel each other.

One way lightning is created is when electrons pile up at the bottom of a cloud. They carry a strong negative charge. That charge repels electrons on the earth's surface just below the cloud, creating an area that is positively charged. Then, electrons from the cloud flow toward the earth in a strong electric current—lightning—because opposites attract.

Static electricity is electricity on a much smaller scale than lightning. An electric charge collects on an object rather than flowing through it as a current. If you walk across a carpet on a dry, winter day, you pick up extra electrons. Those extra electrons look for a positive charge in order to find balance. When they find the positive charge on your dog, you feel a little shock or spark of electricity.

Remembering Friction, Forgetting Friction

Friction is a force that resists motion between two surfaces that touch each other.

Two rough surfaces moving past each other have more friction than two smooth surfaces. Friction is the enemy of motion, but it's not all bad. Friction helps our car tires "grip" the road and our shoes "stick" to the sidewalk. If there were no force resisting the motion, our cars would slip on the road and our feet would slither on the sidewalk. On the other hand, we want our playground slides to be smooth and slippery so that we don't stop on the way down.

Racing Through Space

Relative motion is motion observed from different points of view.

Different observers will see motion differently. Let's say our first observer is a mom. She sees a child riding a bicycle with a dog in the bike's basket. They appear to be moving a few miles per hour. But let's say there's another observer at the center of the earth. This observer sees the child and dog move at roughly the same speed as the rotating earth, which is very fast—about 1,000 miles per hour. A third observer on the sun will see the child and dog move at an even faster speed, or about 67,000 miles per hour. That's how fast the earth moves as it orbits the sun.

Reflecting on a Star

Reflection of light is when light bounces off the surface of an object or body. The light is not absorbed.

Starlight can be reflected (bounced back) or refracted (bent) by the earth's atmosphere. It strikes air molecules and is bounced and bent in many directions. This makes the star's brightness vary, which makes the star twinkle. A star close to the horizon appears to twinkle more than higher stars. This is because there are more air molecules between the star near the horizon and us. Our own eyes (and a dog's eyes) can reflect light, and this reflection is what others see as a twinkle in your eyes.

Our Place in the Universe

Paradox is a statement that seems to contradict itself but might be true anyway.

The universe is so huge, we sometimes feel like a tiny, insignificant part of it. But in our own world of family and friends, we are near the center. To put it another way, we are both insignificant and important at the same time. That's a delightful puzzle, or paradox. The world is full of such mysteries. The scientist Albert Einstein showed that light is a wave, but it's also a particle. How can it be both? Curious people are still exploring our world and discovering new things all the time.

For kids and dogs who race through space every day —*LWP*
Thank you, Laura —*SB*

Acknowledgments:

Many thanks to Melissa Hedwall, physics instructor at Highland Park Senior High School, St. Paul, Minnesota; Justin Spencer, director of education, The Bakken Museum, Minneapolis; Bill Robbins, friend and retired materials scientist for 3M; and my tireless editor Rebecca Davis —*LWP*

Wordsong
An imprint of Astra Books for Young Readers,
a division of Astra Publishing House
astrapublishinghouse.com
Printed in China

ISBN: 978-1-63592-527-2 (hc)
ISBN: 978-1-63592-546-3 (eBook)
Library of Congress Control Number: 2021925706

First edition
10 9 8 7 6 5 4 3 2 1

Design by Barbara Grzeslo
The text is set in Frutiger 55.
The titles are set in Frutiger 75.
The drawings are done in pen and ink and digitally colored.

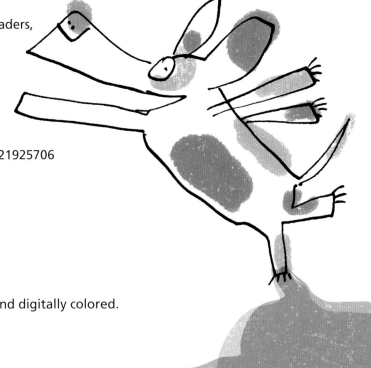